The Berenstain Bears®
BE YOUR BEST BEAR!

The Berenstain Bears®
BE YOUR BEST BEAR!
Stan & Jan Berenstain

Random House New York

Contents

The Berenstain Bears
and the
HOMEWORK HASSLE

If you're a bear for TV,
loud music, and fun,
how ya gonna get
your homework done?

Mama was sitting in her favorite chair straightening up her sewing basket when she sniffed the air and said, "What's that funny smell?"

Papa looked up from the evening paper and sampled the air. "Hmmm," he said. "I smell it, too. It smells like ..."

"Garbage!" said Mama. "It smells like garbage."

Papa sniffed again. "Now, where do you suppose ..."

"I'll tell you where I suppose!" said Mama, who had put aside her sewing basket and sniffed around the room. "It's coming from Brother's backpack."

And sure enough, it was. There was an old banana peel, a brown apple core, and a moldy piece of bread in Brother's backpack.

But that wasn't all there was in Brother's backpack. Among the books and papers was a letter. It was old and wrinkled, and it was from his teacher. Mama read it.

Then she passed it to Papa. After Papa read it, he looked across the table at Brother, who was doing his homework.

At least, he was *supposed* to be doing his homework. And maybe he was. But it was hard to tell by looking at him. He had a card table set up in front of the television, which was showing his favorite program, *The Bear Stooges*. He was listening to his boom box and talking into a cell phone at the same time. There was a Game Bear and a bowl of popcorn on the TV. And, oh yes, there were some school books and a paper and pencil, too.

"Excuse me, young sir," said Papa. "Is this the Mars space station?"

"I'll get back to you, Fred," said Brother.

He put down the cell phone and turned off the boom box. "I'm not quite reading you, Dad."

"You're not reading much of anything, according to this letter from your teacher. You may as well have *been* on Mars for all the attention you've been paying to your homework lately," said Papa.

"Letter? What letter?" asked Brother.

"This old, wrinkled letter that Mama found in your backpack," said Papa. The letter may have been old and wrinkled, but its message was clear.

Dear Parent,
I regret to report that Brother Bear has fallen too far behind in his homework. Please call me.
Yours truly
Teacher Bob

"In my backpack?" said Brother. "I thought my backpack was private."

"When something starts to smell like garbage," said Mama, "it isn't private anymore."

Sister Bear couldn't resist putting her two cents in. "I don't see how you expect Brother to keep up with his homework. He has so many more *interesting* things to do. There's soccer, basketball, video games, going around like a big shot, and *girls*."

Brother turned on Sister. "Why, you little . . . !"

"That will be quite enough, Sister," said Papa. "Why don't you go do your own homework?"

"It's all done," said Sister. "See?"

"You call those scribbles homework, you little twerp?" shouted Brother.

"Now," said Mama, "let's everyone calm down and try to figure out what the problem is."

"I'll tell you what the problem is! The problem is too much homework! Vocabulary homework! Arithmetic homework! Science homework! It's homework, homework, homework! Every subject! Every day till it's coming out of my ears!"

"Uh-huh," said Papa. "Tell me, son, what is your homework for today?"

"Adding and subtracting fractions and memorizing two stanzas of 'The Bear Stood on the Burning Deck.'"

"That really doesn't seem like too much homework to me, son," said Papa.

Brother slumped and stared at the Bear Stooges, who were busy hitting one another on the head.

"I'm not hearing any sort of explanation," said Papa. "I guess that's because tonight's homework isn't really the problem. The problem is that you haven't been handing in your homework on a daily basis. You haven't been taking care of business. You've been falling behind."

"Gee, what's going to happen?" asked Brother as the living room phone rang.

"It's the BRS," said Mama. "For you, Papa."

"Take their number and I'll call them back," said Papa.

"What's the BRS, Mama?" asked Sister.

"It's the Bears' Revenue Service," said Mama. "They collect taxes."

"What's going to happen," said Papa, "is that there's not going to be any more Mars space station. No more boom box. No more popcorn. It's just you and your homework until you're all caught up."

"But that'll take forever!" moaned Brother.
"Nevertheless," said Papa.

"You just don't understand!" said Brother, heading for the door.
"Where are you going?" asked Mama.

"I'm just going for a walk," said Brother.

As often happened when Brother had a problem and went for a walk, his feet led him to Gramps and Gran's, just down the road.

Gramps and Gran could tell Brother was in trouble as soon as they opened the door. After some milk and cookies, Brother told them the whole miserable story: the telltale letter, the missed assignments, the no television, the no video games, the no anything until he caught up. And he was so far behind that he'd never catch up.

"Oh, you'll catch up," said Gramps. "Your father did."

"Huh?" said Brother.

"Same thing happened with your dad when he was your age," said Gramps. "Of course, there was no television then."

No television, thought Brother. Wow! That would have been like *really* being on Mars!

"We had radio," continued Gramps. "We still have it, of course. But radio was like television then. It had great stories every evening. There was a Western called *Bearsmoke,* and *Buck Bruin in the Twenty-Fifth Century* was sort of like *Bear Trek* is now. And your dad listened to them while he did his homework. And he was big on sports, just as you are. So he fell further and further behind. I clamped down on him, just the way he's clamping down on you."

Gee, thought Brother. Papa *does* understand. The thought that he'd gone through it all himself made Brother feel a little bit better.

A stranger was meeting with Papa
when Brother got home.
"He's from the BRS," said Sister.
"It has something to do with taxes. It
looks like Papa hasn't been taking
care of business, either."

The stranger was about to leave.

"We'll be glad to give you a little more time. But you're going to have to catch up," he said as he left.

And that's how it worked out. Brother
sat on one side of the card table, and Papa
sat on the other side.
  It was a good lesson for both of them.

The Berenstain Bears
FORGET THEIR
MANNERS

"Please" and "Thank you"
Help quite a lot
To make a polite bear
Out of one who is not.

Etiquette
for
Bears

There was trouble in the big tree house down a sunny dirt road deep in Bear Country—trouble with manners. The Bear family's trouble with manners was that they *forgot* them!

At first it was just an occasional "please" or "thank you" that was forgotten.

Then there was a rude push without an "excuse me."

Then a reach across the table instead
of a "please pass the broccoli."

Mama Bear wasn't quite sure how or why it happened. But she was sure of one thing—whatever the reason, the Bear family had become a pushing, shoving, name-calling, ill-mannered mess!

SILLYHEAD!

FUZZBRAIN!

NOODLEPUSS!

At the table it was even worse. They were a grabbing, mouth-stuffing, food-fighting, kicking-under-the-table super mess!

Of course, Mama Bear tried to correct Brother and Sister Bear's behavior.

She tried coaxing.

She tried complaining.

She tried shouting!

She tried going to Papa for help (though it sometimes seemed to Mama that he was part of the problem).

Papa banged on the table and shouted as only he could shout. But nothing really seemed to do any good.

Mama didn't like what was happening to her family. Not one bit. Something had to be done. But what? The best way to fight *bad* habits, she thought, was with *good* habits. Then she thought of a plan. She got a big piece of cardboard and a marker. At the top she wrote:

THE BEAR FAMILY POLITENESS PLAN

HOME
SWEET
TREE

THE BEAR FAMILY
POLITENESS PLAN

When the plan was finished, she called a family meeting and showed it to Papa and the cubs.

It certainly got the Bear family's attention!

THE BEAR FAMILY POLITENESS PLAN

RUDENESS	PENALTY
FORGETTING "PLEASE" OR "THANK YOU"	SWEEP FRONT STEPS
PUSHING OR SHOVING	BEAT 2 RUGS
INTERRUPTING	DUST DOWNSTAIRS
NAME CALLING	CLEAN CELLAR
REACHING AT TABLE	CLEAN YARD
PLAYING WITH FOOD	WASH DISHES
RUDE NOISES	WEED GARDEN
BANGING DOOR	CLEAN ATTIC
FORGETTING "EXCUSE ME"	EMPTY GARBAGE
HOGGING BATHROOM	PUT OUT TRASH

Mama's plan had a list of all the rude things she wanted to stop. Beside each one was a penalty—a job or chore that went with it. If you forgot a "please" or a "thank you," you had to sweep the front steps. If you pushed or shoved, you had to beat two rugs. If you got caught name calling, you had to clean the whole cellar!

"But, Mama!" sputtered the cubs. "You're not being fair!"

"It seems to me," she said, "that *you're* the ones who aren't being fair—to yourselves or anyone else. That's what manners are all about—being fair and considerate. Manners are very important. They help us get along with each other. Why, without manners—"

"Your mama's absolutely right!" interrupted Papa.

"Thank you, Papa, for your comment. But interrupting is number three on the Rude List, and the penalty is dusting the downstairs," Mama said, and handed him the feather duster.

"Hmm," said Brother. "This looks serious.
I think we'd better come up with a plan of
our own or we're going to be doing a lot
of extra chores."

"What sort of plan?" asked Sister.

"Well," he said, "instead of just being
polite, we'll be *super* polite. We'll
'please' and 'thank you' so much that
Mama will get fed up and call the whole
thing off!"

"Yes," said Sister. "We'll be so polite,
she won't be able to stand it!"

They put their plan into action.
They were super polite...

—on the stairs:
"After you, Sister dear!"
"Thank you, dear Brother!"

—in the hall:
"Excuse me, Brother dear!"
"Why, certainly, my dear Sister!"

—waiting for the bathroom:

"Terribly sorry to have kept you waiting!"

"Think nothing of it, my dear!"

But it didn't work the way they expected.
Mama didn't get fed up at all. And after a
while Brother and Sister forgot about
being super polite and were
just polite . . .

—at the table:
    "Pass the honey,
please."
      "Certainly."

—in their room:
    "Would you like me to
help you pick up your toys?"
    "Thank you very much."

—in the yard:
"Oops! Sorry—I didn't mean to bump you."
"That's all right. No harm done."

And it turned out that Mama had been right: things *did* go more smoothly. Once they got into the good manners habit, they didn't even have to think about it.

But it wasn't so easy for Papa. He was the one who got fed up. It's a little harder to change habits when you're older, and he had to do quite a few extra chores for forgetting his manners.

"I'm glad to get out of the house, away from that Politeness Plan!" he said as he drove the family along the highway on a trip to the supermarket.

"Manners and courtesy are just as important away from home—especially on the road," said Mama as they stopped at a stop sign to let pedestrians and other cars pass. "They help us drive safely."

"Well," grumbled Papa as they all went into the busy supermarket, "I think you can have too much of a good thing— you've got to have common sense along with manners! Why, if you let everyone go ahead of you at the checkout, you'd be there forever!

"And sometimes you *have* to interrupt—
Excuse me, madam," he interrupted a
shopper, "but I believe you have a
leaking bottle in your cart!" The
shopper thanked him for his help.

"You see?" he said, driving home. "There's more to life than remembering your manners. Besides, manners are all right for cubs and mama bears...

"...but we papa bears have other things to think about—" At that moment the car in front stopped suddenly and Papa bumped into it. He was furious. "Why, that pinheaded fiddlebrain!" he snarled.

"Name calling!" reminded Sister.

BONK!

B.BEARS

The penalty for name calling was cleaning the whole cellar, so Papa gritted his teeth and remembered his manners. And a good thing, too. Because climbing out of the other car was the biggest, angriest bear he had ever seen!

But when the angry bear saw how polite
Papa was, he remembered his manners too. He
explained that he had stopped short because a
mama duck and her ducklings had crossed in front
of him. Then he and Papa Bear looked at their
bumpers and saw that no harm had been done.

"As I was saying," said Papa as they continued on their way, "it's very important for us to remember our manners at all times—and I want to thank you, Sister, for reminding me to remember mine."

"You're very welcome, I'm sure," said Sister Bear politely.

The Berenstain Bears
LEARN ABOUT
STRANGERS

Bear Country is safe
When every small cub there
Learns some special lessons
From ma and papa bear.

Brother and Sister Bear, who lived with their mama and papa in the big tree house down a sunny dirt road deep in Bear Country, looked quite a lot alike.

Except for the fact that Brother was a boy cub and Sister was a girl cub, they *were* alike in many ways. And even though they each had hobbies (Brother loved to build and fly model airplanes; Sister had all sorts of special interests), they enjoyed many of the same things: bike riding, baseball, soccer, Frisbee, and just getting out and enjoying nature.

Yes, Brother and Sister were alike in many ways.
But in some important ways they were different.

Brother Bear was cautious and careful
and a little wary of strangers. Sister,
on the other hand, wasn't the least bit
wary. She was friendly to a fault.
Just about everybody
that came her way got a
big hello.

"Hello, butterfly!"

Brother worried about Sister's free and easy way with strangers. Strangers weren't a problem for him. Not talking to strangers suited cautious and careful Brother just fine. But friendly-to-a-fault Sister was different. She talked to *everybody*.

"Sister," said Brother. "You're going to have to stop that!"

"Stop what?" she asked.

"Talking to strangers! It's just not a good idea!"

"Why?" she wanted to know. "Why shouldn't I talk to strangers? What harm is there in it? Is there something *wrong* with strangers?"

"Hmm," said Brother, thinking about it for a moment. "Those aren't questions for a brother. Those are for a mama or papa...."

"Sister Bear, I'm glad you asked those questions!" said Papa Bear, in his deepest and most serious voice. "The reason you should never talk to a stranger and never *ever* take presents from a stranger and never *ever* *ever* go anywhere with a stranger is that it's dangerous."

"What's dangerous about it?" she asked, wide-eyed. "What can happen?"

Oh, dear, thought Mama Bear. I *do* hope Papa can tell Sister about strangers without making everything scary.

"All sorts of things!" Papa said. "Here! Look at the newspaper!"

As she looked at it her eyes got wider and wider.

This is what she saw. . . .

"I hope you're paying attention to all this," called Papa to Brother Bear.

"Yes, Papa," said Brother, looking up from his airplanes.

When Sister asked for a bedtime story that evening, Papa said, "Of course! I have just the one!"

It was in an old book that Papa had kept since he was a cub. The story was called "Silly Goose and Wily Fox." It told how Silly Goose got into a conversation with Wily Fox, and before Silly knew quite what was happening she found herself in Wily's lair. This is how the story ended:

"'…then there was a snip and a snap and all that was left of Silly Goose was a few floating feathers and a smile on the face of Wily Fox.'"

Sister had a hard time falling asleep that night. Her mind was filled with those headlines. There was even one that said SILLY GOOSE MISSING! WILY FOX QUESTIONED!

STRANGER BOTHERS CUB
MISSING CUB FOUND
CHIEF GRIZZLY
SILLY GOOSE
QUESTIONS
MISSING
STRANGER
WILY FOX
QUESTIONED

The sound of Brother Bear's peaceful breathing finally lulled her to sleep.

The next day dawned bright and friendly—to everybody but Sister. She had spent a restless night and when she looked out the window, everything seemed a little strange. The trees seemed to reach for her, an owl stared at her, and the crows glared.

"Let's go out and ride our bikes on the village green!" said Brother after breakfast. But Sister didn't want to. Brother was puzzled. The green was a bright, busy, friendly place where she loved to play.

"Well, how about some soccer?" But she didn't want to do that either.

It wasn't until he suggested Frisbee, her favorite game, that she agreed to go along.

Before they left, they told Mama where they'd be—it was a family rule that they never went anywhere without telling Mama or Papa.

"That's fine," said Mama. "I'm on my way to Farmer Ben's for apples. I'll stop by for you on the way home."

The village green was the same bustling place it had always been. This is what it looked like—*to everyone but Sister.*

This is what it looked like to her. Today even the frogs and butterflies seemed mean and scary to Sister.

Later, when somebody tapped her on the shoulder, she jumped a mile—even though it was just Mama.

"How was everything at the village green?" asked Mama on the way home in the car. Sister sat in front with Mama, and Brother rode in back with the barrel of apples.

"All right, I guess," said Sister. "But there were so many *strangers*!"

Later at home, when Mama and Sister were getting ready to make applesauce, Mama said, "You know, what Papa told you was quite right. It's *not* a good idea to talk to strangers or accept presents or rides from them.

"But," she continued, *"that doesn't mean that all strangers are bad.* Why, chances are, there wasn't a single person on that green that would harm a fly, much less a fine little cub like you. The trouble is . . . well, it's like this barrel of apples. There's an old saying that goes, 'There'll always be a couple of bad apples in every barrel.' That's the way it is with strangers. Cubs have to be careful because of the few 'bad apples.'"

"Look!" said Sister. "I found one! It's all bumpy and has a funny shape!"

"Well, it certainly is strange looking," said Mama. "But that doesn't necessarily mean it's bad. You can't always tell from the outside which are the 'bad apples.'"

She cut it in half. "See?" she said. "It's fine inside."

"Now, here's one that looks fine on the outside ...

—but inside, it's all wormy."

"Yugh!" said Sister.

"What's up?" asked Brother.

"A bad apple!" said Sister.

"Double yugh!" said Brother. "Hey! I'm going to the meadow to fly my new pusher plane. Want to come?"

"Sure," Sister said. "I can pick some wildflowers!" She felt much better now—more like her old friendly self.

The pusher plane was a great success, and the cubs were about to head home when someone drove onto the meadow with a big beautiful orange and green model airplane.

"Wait!" said Brother. "I want to watch! It's a radio-controlled job!"

Sister went back to picking wildflowers, but before she knew it, Brother was *talking to the stranger*! For that's what he was, a stranger—no matter how big and beautiful his radio-controlled job was!

She dropped her wildflowers and ran over to them.

"I'm going to send it up and follow
in the car," the stranger was saying.
"Want to come along?"

"Wow!" said Brother. And he *would*
have—if Sister hadn't grabbed his arm
and said, "Don't you dare!"

The stranger drove off following his airplane, and Sister ran home shouting, "Brother talked to a stranger! Brother talked to a stranger!"

"But it was a big orange and green radio-controlled job!" said Brother.

"That doesn't matter," said Papa. "We have rules about strangers— and they're important!"

"We have rules about tattletales, too," said Brother, glaring at Sister.

"Sister wasn't tattling. Tattling is telling just to be mean," explained Mama. "And Sister was telling because she loves you and was worried."

"Do you think that fellow was a 'bad apple'?" asked Brother.

"Probably not," said Mama.

"That's right," said Sister. "Most folks are friendly and nice and wouldn't hurt a fly. But *you have to be careful, just in case.*"

"Speaking of apples," said Mama, "how about some of this applesauce I just made?"

As they sat having a dish of Mama's delicious applesauce, Brother and Sister thought about what they had learned that day. There was quite a lot to think about.

For Brother and Sister's Rules for Cubs, turn the page.

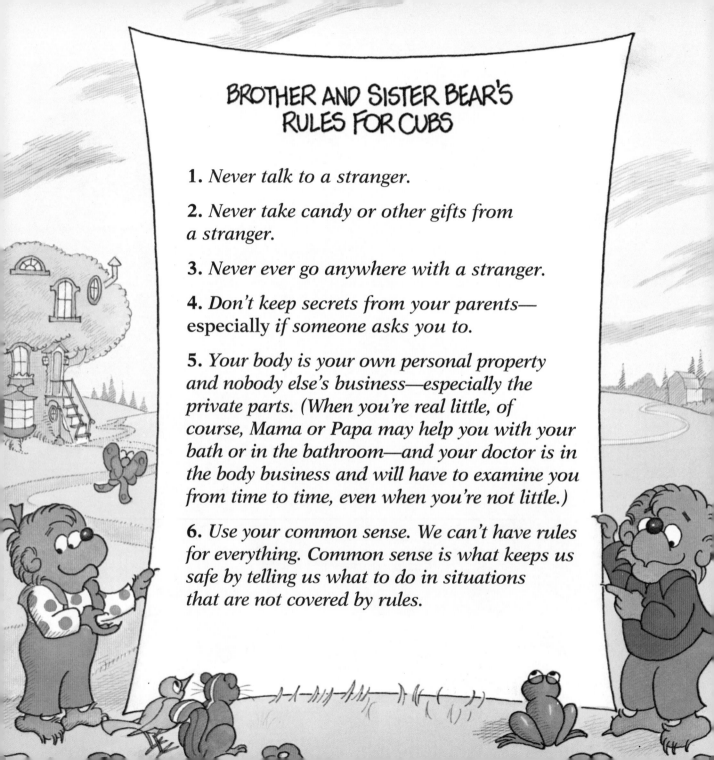

BROTHER AND SISTER BEAR'S RULES FOR CUBS

1. *Never talk to a stranger.*

2. *Never take candy or other gifts from a stranger.*

3. *Never ever go anywhere with a stranger.*

4. *Don't keep secrets from your parents— especially if someone asks you to.*

5. *Your body is your own personal property and nobody else's business—especially the private parts. (When you're real little, of course, Mama or Papa may help you with your bath or in the bathroom—and your doctor is in the body business and will have to examine you from time to time, even when you're not little.)*

6. *Use your common sense. We can't have rules for everything. Common sense is what keeps us safe by telling us what to do in situations that are not covered by rules.*

The Berenstain Bears
and the MESSY ROOM

When small bears forget
To pick up, store and stash,
Some of their favorite things
End up in the trash.

From the outside, the Bears' tree house, which stood beside a sunny dirt road deep in Bear Country, looked very neat and well-kept.

The flower beds sparkled with red, yellow, and blue tulips.

The woodwork was freshly painted and in good repair.

The grass was cut and the vegetable patch was properly weeded.

Even the bird's nest that perched on one of the tree house branches was well-trimmed.

The inside of the Bears'
tree house was neat and clean too.

The pictures were straight.

The piano was dusted.

The kitchen was spick-and-span.

Even the basement was neat and clean.
(And if you think it's easy to keep a
tree house basement neat and clean—
well, you've never tried to do it!)

Yes, the Bears' tree house was a lesson in neatness and cleanliness.

Except for one place...

Brother Bear and Sister Bear's room.
IT...WAS...A...*MESS*!!!

A dust-catching, wall-to-wall, helter-skelter mess!

A half-done jigsaw puzzle gathered dust in one corner of the room.

A group of Brother's dinosaur models collected cobwebs in another.

Sister's stuffed animals were everywhere.

It wasn't that Brother and Sister were naturally messy. They *tried* to keep their room straight.

They made their beds...

most of the time,

and they swept
and picked up ...

once in a while.

The trouble was that when clean-up time came, they spent more time arguing than cleaning.

"How am *I* supposed to sweep with your dumb dinosaur toys all over the floor?" argued Sister.

"They're not toys—they're *models*! And don't move them! I'm working on a set-up of the Pleistocene Age!" Brother protested.

"Pleistocene schmeistocene!" shouted Sister.

Not only was Brother and Sister's room a mess, but Brother and Sister were getting to be a mess too—always arguing about clean-up chores instead of sharing the job and working as a team.

What usually happened was that while the cubs
argued about whose turn it was to do what,
Mama took the broom and did the sweeping herself...

and she often did the picking up too.
That was the worst part—the picking up.

And the putting away.

Well, the mess just seemed to build up and build up, until one day...maybe it was because Mama's back was a little stiff, or maybe it was stepping on Brother's airplane cement, or maybe she was just fed up with that messy room, but whatever it was...Mama Bear lost her temper!

She stormed into the
cubs' room with a big box.

"The first thing we have to do is get rid of all this junk!" she said.

"*JUNK!?*" said Brother and Sister, watching in horror as Mama began to throw things into the box.

"My Teddy isn't junk!" screamed Sister.

"My bird's nest collection isn't junk!" yelled Brother at the top of his lungs.

The screaming and yelling got so loud that it reached Papa, who was in his workshop putting the finishing touches on a batch of chairs that had been ordered by one of his customers. He couldn't imagine what was wrong.

He hurried up the stairs and looked into the messy, *noisy* room. It didn't take a deep thinker to figure out what was going on.

Papa got Mama's and the cubs'
attention and called a family meeting
right then and there.

"Now, the mess has really built up in this
room," he said. "In fact, it's the worst case
of messy build-up I've ever seen!
"And it isn't fair," he continued. "It isn't
fair to your mama and me, because we have a lot
of other things to take care of. And it isn't
fair to you, because you really can't have fun
or relax in a room that's such a terrible mess."

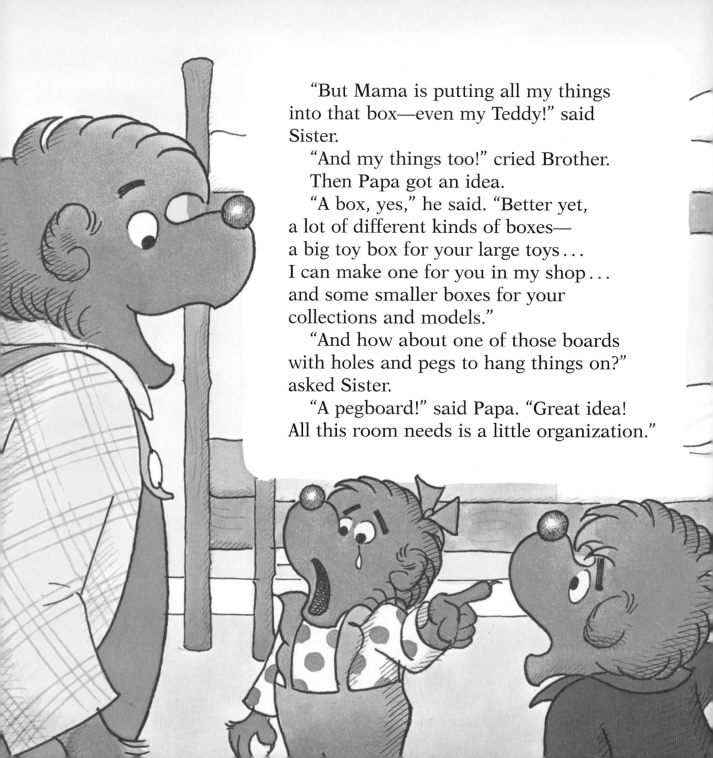

"But Mama is putting all my things into that box—even my Teddy!" said Sister.

"And my things too!" cried Brother.

Then Papa got an idea.

"A box, yes," he said. "Better yet, a lot of different kinds of boxes— a big toy box for your large toys... I can make one for you in my shop... and some smaller boxes for your collections and models."

"And how about one of those boards with holes and pegs to hang things on?" asked Sister.

"A pegboard!" said Papa. "Great idea! All this room needs is a little organization."

"A little organization—*and* a few rules!" added Mama. "Rules about more sweeping and less arguing and not leaving things to gather dust and cobwebs."

Papa set to work making a fine big toy box and a large pegboard...

while the cubs and Mama
sorted out toys, books, games,
and puzzles and put them
into boxes that fit neatly
into the closet.
Every box was
clearly labeled.

Some of the cubs' things did end up in Mama's big throwaway box— not Sister's Teddy, of course, but some of Brother's bird's nests (the crumbling, falling-apart ones).

It was a very big job cleaning up all that messy build-up. But after a lot of straightening up and putting away, the job was finally finished.

"Wow!" said Brother. "That was quite a job, but it was worth it!"

"It looks like a whole new room!" said Sister.

The cubs were right.

TOYS

And Papa had been right too. It was so much more enjoyable to live in a neat, clean, well-organized room— and so much more relaxing!

It wasn't as exciting to open the big storage closet now, but it was much more practical—and a lot more fun!

The Berenstain Bears
and
THE TRUTH

No matter how you hope,
No matter how you try,
You can't make truth
Out of a lie.

It was a lazy sort of day in Bear Country. The air was so still that the leaves on the big tree house where the Bear family lived were hardly rustling.

Except in the beehive, where the bees were always busy, nothing much seemed to be happening.

It was the sort of day that sometimes leads to mischief.

Inside the tree house Brother and Sister
Bear were sitting around not doing anything
in particular.

Brother was holding his soccer ball—he'd
become interested in soccer and had been outside
practicing free kicks. Sister was relaxing in
an easy chair, thinking about what to do next.

Neither Papa nor Mama Bear was around. Papa was in his shop working on some furniture, and Mama was out shopping.

"I know what," said Sister. "Let's go gather some wild blackberries."

Brother thought about that.

"No," he said, "wild black-berries have too many thorns, and besides, the seeds get stuck in your teeth."

"Well, then," said Sister, "let's go out and twist each other up on the swing and see who gets the dizziest."

Brother thought about that.

"No," he said. "That's silly, and besides, we did that yesterday."

Sister became irritated and impatient with her brother.

"My goodness!" she complained. "You don't want to do *anything*. All you want to do is sit there and hug that soccer ball. I think you must be in love with that soccer ball!"

"I am not!" protested Brother.
"But I'll tell you something—I bet
I can dribble this ball past you!"

Brother was a pretty good soccer player
and a *very* good dribbler. But so was Sister.

The only one who saw what happened next, besides the cubs, was a mockingbird who was perched on a twig outside an open window.

Brother faced Sister. The ball was on the floor between them. First Brother moved the ball with his right foot,

then with his left, trying to trick Sister out of position.

Then, quick as a flash, he gave the ball a sharp kick with his right.

It almost worked.
But Sister was fast too. She reached
out with her knee and blocked the ball,

which bounced against a bookshelf,

against a chair,

against a footstool,

and into Mama's *most favorite* lamp,

which fell to the floor with a crash!

The mockingbird let out a screech and got out of there as fast as its wings could carry it. As it flew away it saw Mama Bear returning from the marketplace!

Now, the Bear family had some house rules just as any family has. One was "No honey eating in bed." Another was "No tracking mud on the clean floors." And another was *"No ball playing in the house!"*

What to do? Brother looked at Sister. Sister looked at Brother. They both looked at the broken lamp. And they both listened in horror as Mama came up the front steps and into the house.

All Brother had time to do before Mama came into the room was roll the ball behind Papa's chair.

"My lamp!" said Mama. "My best lamp! What happened?" she asked, looking into her cubs' eyes. "Tell me about it."

The cubs looked into Mama's eyes, then at each other, and then they began to tell one of the biggest whoppers that has ever been told in Bear Country.

"It was a bird!" began Brother.
"Yes," added Sister, "a big purple
bird with yellow feet!"

"And green wing tips,"
added Brother.

"And funny-looking red
feathers sticking out of its
head," said Sister, as a
finishing touch.

As most lies do, the purple bird
whopper got bigger and bigger and bigger.

"Yes," continued the cubs, "and it flew in that window, zoomed around the room, and knocked over the lamp!"

As Mama Bear was looking at the broken lamp with a sad expression on her face, Papa Bear came in from his shop.

The cubs began to tell him the story of the big bird that flew in the window and broke the lamp. It was harder to tell the second time. For one thing, they couldn't quite remember how they had told it the first time.

"You've got me confused," said Papa. "Was it a purple bird with green wing tips and yellow feet?

"Or a yellow bird with purple wing tips and green feet?

"*Or* . . . was it a white bird with black spots . . .

like that soccer ball behind my easy chair?"

But the thing that really made it hard the second time was how very sad Mama looked as she picked up the pieces of the broken lamp.

"Mama, we're really sorry about the lamp," said Brother.

"Oh, yes!" said Sister, picking up the last piece and putting it in the dust pan.

"Oh," said Mama, "I'm not worried about the lamp. We can always get another lamp, or we can glue this one back together. What I'm sad about is the thought that maybe, just maybe, my cubs, whom I've always trusted, aren't telling me the truth. And trust is not something you can put back together again."

Both cubs started to talk at once.
"It wasn't a bird!" said Sister. "It was
a soccer ball."
"And it was all my fault!" shouted Brother.
"It was just as much my fault!" shouted
Sister.

But they were both shouted down by
the phone, which rang loudly.

It was Grizzly Gran
inviting the Bear family
for a Sunday visit.

"Hello, Gran!" said Mama. "Oh, everything
is just fine here in the tree house. How is
everything with you?"

"But, Mama!" protested Sister after Mama
hung up the phone. "You told Gran that everything is fine here, and that isn't really the truth."

"Oh, but it is," answered Mama. "We've got two fine cubs who have just learned a very important lesson about telling the truth. And what could be finer than that?

"Now, let's help Papa glue the lamp back together."

Nobody really expects cubs to be perfect, and from time to time Brother and Sister Bear did forget the rules.

Brother ate honey in bed a couple of times.

One time Sister tracked a little mud on the clean floor.

And once or twice Brother and Sister started to play ball in the house before they remembered not to.

But they never, ever again told a whopper . . .

because trust is one thing you can't put back
together once it's broken.

The Berenstain Bears
and
TOO MUCH TV

When the TV is on
All day without rest,
Mama knows it's too much—
And Mama knows best.

It was a fine spring day in Bear Country. The bluebirds were singing. The trout were leaping. And except for one small cloud of dust billowing behind the school bus as it came over the hill, the air was sparkling clean.

Mama Bear was inside the family's tree house fixing Brother and Sister Bear's after-school snack.

Brother and Sister Bear got off the school bus and came into the kitchen with hardly a hello. Then they did what they did every day: They took their milk and cookies into the living room and switched on the TV.

There's no question about it, thought Mama. Those cubs are watching too much TV!

Later, when Papa Bear came in from his shop and joined Brother and Sister, Mama became even more convinced....

There's absolutely no question about it. The whole Bear family is watching too much TV!

She wasn't quite sure how it had happened. Maybe it began when their old TV broke down and they got a new large-screen model.

Or maybe it started when Papa began tinkering with new gadgets that brought in programs from all over Bear Country.

But however it had happened, one thing was sure—the Bear family was spending more and more time watching television and less and less time with all the other things they might be doing instead.

The Bear family had always had lively conversations around the dinner table—

—but not lately. Lately they just sat around and chewed.

The cubs had all kinds of fun playing outdoors. But not anymore.

They were too busy watching *Nutty Bear* and *The Bear Stooges*.

That evening after dinner, when Brother and Sister scampered in to turn on the TV, Mama stopped them and said her piece: "We've been watching altogether too much television around here!"

"But, Mama," said Brother. "*Nutty Bear* is coming on and we'll miss it!"

"And *The Bear Stooges*!" added Sister.

"Well, you'll just have to miss them!" said Mama firmly.

"And furthermore," she added, "you may as well get used to the idea because there's *not going to be any television around here for a whole week!*"

"No TV for a week!?" said the shocked cubs. "But, Mama..."

"Never mind the *buts*," said Papa. "Your mother is absolutely right. There's a lot more to life than TV—like homework, for instance. And fresh air and sunshine. And exercise. No TV for a week is an excellent idea....

"Now, if you'll excuse me, there's a sports show I want to watch."

"Just a moment, Papa," said Mama. "No TV for a week means you, too."

"What?!" said Papa. "You can't be serious!"

But Mama was very serious.

"What about the news?" protested Papa. "I won't know what's going on in the world if I don't watch the TV news!"

"Here, try this," said Mama. "It's called the newspaper."

"And the weather!" continued Papa. "How will we know what the weather will be?"

"Try this," said Mama. "It's
called putting your hand out the
window to see if it's raining."
"What are we supposed to
do—just sit around and
talk?" asked Brother.
"That'll be fine for
starters," said Mama,
settling comfortably
into her rocker.

But it had been so long since the Bear family sat around and talked that they had sort of forgotten how.

It really didn't matter, because pretty soon Papa fell asleep and snored so loudly that they wouldn't have heard each other anyway.

After school the next day, the cubs looked longingly at the TV but Mama shooed them out to play.

Brother's bike had a tire that needed pumping up and Sister's trike needed a little oil—and while it seemed strange not watching television, it was fun riding bikes and trikes again. Sort of.

That evening the cubs worked on their homework. But it wasn't easy with that blank TV just sitting there staring.

Then Sister noticed an ad in Papa's newspaper—an ad for a special new TV program.

"Oh, Mama!" she said. "Look! A brand-new show!"

"No TV for a week means no TV for a week," answered Mama. "And besides, Mother Nature has a much bigger show waiting for us. We're going to sit outside and watch the stars come out."

"Watch the stars come out?!" complained Sister.

"I don't know if I can stand the excitement," said Brother.

But as they sat out under the great sky, a spell came over the bears. It was all so big and beautiful. The bears stared at the sky. So far, not a single star.

"Look!" cried Sister. "Something flying!"

"Bats," said Papa. "Out for their breakfast of insects."

"Breakfast?" asked Brother.

"That's right," answered Papa. "Bats sleep during the day, so this is their breakfast time."

"I see a star!" cried Sister. She had found the first tiny star.

Soon there were others.

And after a while the whole sky was full of stars.

And it was very special—more special than anything they'd ever seen on TV. It was a sharper picture, too—and a much, much, *much* bigger screen.

The Bear family did all sorts of interesting things over the next few days—so interesting that they hardly thought about TV.

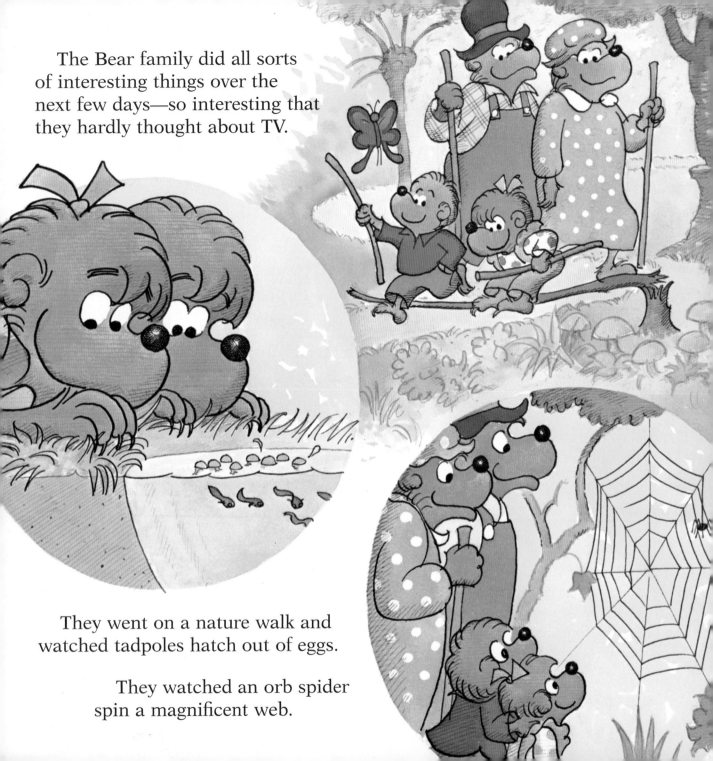

They went on a nature walk and watched tadpoles hatch out of eggs.

They watched an orb spider spin a magnificent web.

They went shopping at the Bear Country Mall. Sister used some of her savings to buy a knitting spool and some yarn. Brother bought a cube puzzle.

They did have to keep an eye on Papa, though.

When they were at the mall, the cubs caught Papa in the TV store sneaking a look at a game show.

Another time he went downstairs in the middle of the night for a peek at the late-late movie, but Mama and the cubs stopped him just in time.

The next evening—it was the last day of their no-TV week—the Bear family was having a lively conversation at the dinner table. They all agreed that the week had been a success, but Brother had a question.

"Mama," he asked, "what is it you don't like about TV? What do you have against it?"

"Goodness," said Mama. "I don't have anything against TV. I like it. What I'm against is the *TV habit*—sitting in front of it day after day like old stumps waiting for dry rot to set in."

"Well," said Brother, "tomorrow I'm going to get a whole bunch of snacks and watch TV all day!"

"Me, too!" said Sister.

"Me, too!" said Papa.

But the only one who did watch it all day was Papa. Brother got interested in his cube puzzle and finally solved it. Sister started knitting a rug on her knitting spool.

Finally even Papa had enough, and decided to bait his hook for a couple of those leaping trout.

All About the Berenstains

Many years ago, when their two sons were beginning to read, Stan and Jan Berenstain created the endearing bear clan that shares their own family name.

After the first book appeared in the 1960s, they wrote and illustrated more than three hundred Berenstain Bears books in a dozen formats, but the most enduring are the stories in the groundbreaking First Time Books® series. These humorous, warmhearted tales of a growing family (the books started with one cub and ended up with three) deal with issues common to all families with children: sibling rivalry, friendship, school, visits to the doctor and dentist, holiday celebrations, time spent together and apart, competition, good manners, and many more.

Each First Time Book® presents a problem that's resolved—usually by Mama and Papa, but sometimes by Brother and Sister—with good sense and, above all, a sense of humor. Lessons are learned and values explained and passed to the next generation, always through the telling of a good story. The Berenstain Bears First Time Books® have sold millions of copies, a testament to their enduring appeal, to the fact that families everywhere can see themselves in the Berenstain Bears—and to the truth that a well-told tale is indeed timeless.